EYEWITNESS ANIMALS

THE STORY OF

EASTER

The Standard Publishing Company, Cincinnati, Ohio
A division of Standex International Corporation
© 1997 by The Standard Publishing Company
All rights reserved. Printed in the United States of America.
Library of Congress Catalog Card Number 96-38394
04 03 02 01 00 99 98 97   5 4 3 2 1

Designed by Coleen Davis
Graphic layout by Dale Meyers
Edited by Greg Holder

EYEWITNESS ANIMALS

THE STORY OF
EASTER

written by
Robin Currie

illustrated by
Max Kolding

STANDARD PUBLISHING
Cincinnati, Ohio

For Philip Ramsey – pastor, mentor, friend

Contents

One week long ago, many exciting things happened in Jerusalem. It all began with a big parade, led by a little donkey.

Clip-clop Donkey

Hello! My name is Clip-clop Donkey.

Hee-haw!

I want to tell you about the time I led a big parade.

The day started out like any other. Early that morning, Mama Donkey and I walked through the streets of Jerusalem.

Clip-clop, clip-clop.

We ate some green grass.

Chomp, chomp.

Suddenly I heard something

that made my ears perk up.

Touch your ears.

"We want to borrow Clip-clop

for our friend Jesus to ride,"

some men said to my owner.

"No!" I said. I shook my head.

Shake your head.

"I don't want to go,"

I told Mama Donkey.

"I've never given anybody

a ride before. I don't know how.

And who is this Jesus? Where will I

take him?" The men led us away.

Wave good-bye to Clip-clop Donkey.

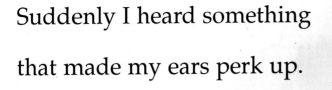

The men were nice to me. They did not make me hurry

or forget to give me a drink of water.

Gulp.

When the men talked more about Jesus,

I perked up my ears again.

Point to your ears.

"Remember when Jesus stopped the storm

on the sea?" one asked.

Blow hard like the wind. Then STOP.

"I sure do," said the other.

"And I remember when Jesus fed five thousand people

with some bread and just two little fish."

Hold up two fingers.

"Humph," I said to Mama Donkey.

"I've never been in a storm, and I *don't* like fish.

Maybe I won't like Jesus."

Then one of the men said, "Look, Clip-clop,

here is something you will like."

And he handed me a crunchy carrot.

Munch and crunch.

"How did these friends of Jesus know I like carrots?"

I asked Mama Donkey between bites.

"Jesus has nice friends. Maybe I *will* like Jesus after all."

One of the men ran ahead.

Tap your hands on your knees to make a running sound.

"Jesus!" he called. "Here is the donkey you wanted."

A man bent down and rubbed my nose.

Rub your nose.

I thought, *This must be Jesus.*

He has a nice smile. I'd like to give him a ride.

So Jesus sat on my back and we set off for Jerusalem.

Make a clip-clop sound.

There were lots of people along the road.

"This must be a parade for someone special,"

I said to Mama Donkey.

People put their coats on the road in front of me

to make a fancy carpet.

Pat the floor.

Some people waved branches from the palm trees.

Wave your hands in the air.

Everyone in Jerusalem was there!

When I saw all the people,

I was excited. Maybe they were

waving and shouting at me! This

was a parade for Clip-clop Donkey!

Point to yourself.

But soon, I knew I was wrong.

The parade was *not* for me.

Shake your head.

The people were shouting,

"Hosanna! Blessed is he who

comes in the name of the Lord!"

Shout "Hosanna!"

"Mama Donkey," I said,

"all the cheering is for *Jesus*.

He must be a king!" I held my head up high.

Hold your head up high and smile.

I carried Jesus all the way to the big temple.

He gave me one more pat on the ears and went up the

steps. Then Mama Donkey nudged me.

"Come on, Clip-clop," she said. "Let's go home."

So we did. But I will always remember

the special day I carried the King.

Hee-haw!

Later that same week, Jesus and his friends had a special meal together. There were no donkeys there, but a little mouse on the floor saw everything.

Whiskers Mouse

Hi, hi, hi! I'm Whiskers Mouse.

Squeak like a little mouse.

Let me tell you about the night

a teacher named Jesus did the work of a servant.

I live with my family inside a house in Jerusalem.

After the people finish eating, I creep out of my hole,

Walk your fingers up your arm.

and I carry away all the crumbs they have dropped.

Then my family has a feast, too.

Clap your hands.

Sometimes I only find brown bread and some rice.

Other times there are sweets and pieces of beef.

Once there was even a wedding cake.

How big do you suppose the cake was?

But on this night, it was a Passover dinner.

First some men came to get things ready.

I told my oldest son, who had come with me,

"I've seen this before.

Tonight is a very special night.

In every house in Jerusalem,

people are eating the very same meal.

And in every house there are mice

ready to lick up some wonderful crumbs!

Rub your tummy.

15

It is called a Passover meal."

I could smell fresh bread baking and a lamb roasting.

Sniff. Yum! Pat your tummy.

I said to my son,

"I've seen this before.

Nod your head.

My family will eat well tonight!"

And I licked my whiskers.

Where would your whiskers be if you were a mouse?

Just before the sun set,

the guests came in, talking and laughing.

They kicked off their sandals and stretched out

on low couches and began to eat dinner.

Now, mice live on the floor,

so we see things that people usually don't see.

Touch your eyes.

I saw dirty feet!

Touch your feet.

Then Jesus called for a bowl of water and a towel.

Soon a servant brought them into the room.

"I've seen this before," I said.

Nod your head.

"The servant is going to wash their feet.

No more dirty feet!"

Hooray for the mice!

But Jesus took the water and towel.

He took off his own robe

and wrapped the towel around himself.

Then he knelt down at the feet

of one of the disciples.

He dipped his hands into the bowl

and rubbed the cool water

all over the disciple's feet.

Rub your feet.

All the talking and laughing stopped.

Jesus kept washing the man's feet with the water.

Then he wiped the feet dry with the towel

and moved on to the next disciple.

I said to my son,

"I've never seen anything like this before!"

Shake your head.

When Jesus had washed the feet of all the men,

they were not dirty anymore.

Much nicer for us mice!

Hooray for the mice!

Jesus put on his robe again and sat down.

He said, "Do you know what I have done?

I've done something you have never seen before.

Shake your head.

I am your teacher,

Point to yourself.

but I did a servant's job because I love you.

Hug yourself.

Now I want you to serve others.

I want you to be a helper like me."

After Jesus finished talking to the disciples,

it was time to finish the meal.

"I've seen this before," I said.

Nod your head.

But on this night, a teacher did the job of a servant because he loved his friends.

Give yourself a hug!

I had never seen *that* before!

Squeak!

**After they sang a song, Jesus and
the disciples went to a garden to pray.
A mouse was too small to go along,
but a dove high in a tree saw everything.**

Flutter Dove

Hello, hello, hello!

Coo, coo.

My name is Flutter Dove.

I want to tell you what happened

one night in a quiet garden outside

of Jerusalem. Well, sometimes it is quiet.

During the day those birds chirp,

cheep, and squawk.

Make a lot of bird sounds: chirp, cheep, squawk.

But in the evening, they all settle down in their nests.

When everything is quiet, it is time

for my friend Twitter and me to coo.

Our song is so soft and quiet,

it puts people to sleep.

Coo, coo, coo.

Sometimes it puts me to sleep, too!

Snore! ZZZZZZZ

No, I'm awake! I'm awake.

Open your eyes wide.

Well, one night, the garden

was getting quiet,

and all the birds were settling down.

I was just about to go to sleep,

when I heard four men entering the garden.

Hold up four fingers.

One man, called Jesus, walked off

to be by himself. I said to Twitter,

"That young man is worried about something.

I can see it on his face."

As I watched from high in my tree,

Jesus looked straight up at me.

I said to Twitter,

"That young man, the worried

one, is talking right to *me*."

Point to yourself.

But then I heard what

Jesus said — "Father, please don't let

this bad thing happen to me."

So he wasn't talking to me at all,

but to God in heaven.

Fold your hands.

He was praying!

I thought to myself,

What kind

of bad thing is going

to happen to Jesus?

He seems like a nice man.

Then Jesus went to talk to his friends.

I flew ahead to where they were waiting for him,

but they were sound asleep!

Rest your head on your hands.

I said, "Coo, coo" as loud as I could to wake them,

Coo really loud.

but the friends were still sleeping.

Rest your head on your hands.

Then Jesus saw them.

He said, "Wake up."

They woke up right away.

Clap your hands.

Jesus said, "I am very sad.

Stay awake and pray with me."

I flew to the tree above him and listened.

This time he said, "Father, not my will, but yours."

He was willing to do things God's way after all.

I said to Twitter,

"Why isn't Jesus worried anymore?"

Twitter said Jesus had talked to God

and now he felt peaceful.

Nod your head.

She was right. The whole garden was peaceful.

Coo, coo, coo.

27

Not for long!

A big crowd of people

came running into the garden.

Tap your hands on your knees fast.

The crowd ran over to Jesus.

Some soldiers grabbed him.

The crowd yelled,

"Get Jesus! Get the king of the Jews."

I said to Twitter,

"That young man who was praying is a king!

Why would the soldiers grab a king?"

But, for once, Twitter did not know the answer.

Shake your head.

Then I looked around for Jesus' friends.

Look around.

They had all run away when the soldiers came.

I said to Twitter,

"Jesus knew that a bad thing would happen,

and he was right. But when the soldiers came,

Jesus wasn't afraid. Why was that?"

Twitter said that Jesus found peace in praying to God.

Fold your hands.

She was right.

Coo, coo.

The soldiers took Jesus away from his friends. There was no place for a dove to sit with all those soldiers around, but a soldier's horse could see everything.

Charger Horse

Hail and greetings! I am Charger Horse.

Whinny!

Can you gallop like a horse?

I belong to a Roman soldier named Marcus.

Let me tell you how he learned the truth about Jesus.

As the horse of an important Roman officer,

I have seen a lot of bad people punished.

But Jesus was different from everyone else.

He never did anything wrong!

Shake your head.

On the day I am remembering,

Marcus was putting my saddle on my back.

Where is your back?

He said to the stableboy,

"Have you heard about Jesus of Nazareth?"

Point to your ears.

"I've heard of him," said the stableboy.

"People say he has healed sick people

and taught about God's love."

Give yourself a hug.

"The Jewish priests are afraid of him," said Marcus.

"They want him to die on the cross."

My leader, Pontius Pilate, put me in charge."

Marcus turned to me and said,

"Come on, Charger. It's time to go."

Pretend to ride Charger the horse.

31

So I galloped up the hill and watched

the soldiers put Jesus on a cross.

I tried not to watch, because it made me sad.

As we stood and waited,

Marcus said to the other soldiers,

"Look at the size of this crowd!

Shade your eyes to look around.

Usually, only a few people come out to watch.

But there is a big crowd to see Jesus."

Then a Jewish priest came walking toward us.

He said, "Who put that sign up there?

It says, 'Jesus of Nazareth, King of the Jews.'"

I started to feel sad for Jesus.

Make a sad face.

I wondered why a good king had to

be treated like this.

Then Jesus said, "Father, forgive them!"

Marcus said to one of the women nearby,

"Did you hear what Jesus just said?

Put your hand up to your ear.

He asked God to forgive the people

who are punishing him!

I've never heard anyone say *that* before."

Marcus watched the face of Jesus

while he gently stroked my mane.

Pretend you are petting Charger.

Then he said to one of the priests,

"Can you believe it?

Jesus is not mad at any of us.

He is trusting God to take care of him.

This Jesus is not like anyone else in the whole world."

Shake your head.

34

Then Jesus shouted,

"Father, I give my life to you."

There was a great big earthquake,

scary lightning, and loud thunder.

Clap real loud.

Then it was over. Jesus had died.

Shh.

In the silence, I heard Marcus say,

"This Jesus really was the Son of God."

Marcus had changed his mind.

Now he knew the truth about Jesus.

Nod your head.

A man named Joseph took Jesus down from the cross.

Jesus' friends carried his body to a cave

on the far side of a garden.

Then Joseph pushed a big, heavy stone

in front of the cave.

Pretend to push something heavy.

No one would be able to go in or out.

On that sad day outside of Jerusalem,

Marcus and I learned the truth about Jesus.

He was not like anybody else in the world.

Shake your head.

Jesus was the Son of God.

Whinny.

Three days later, the stone was moved and something wonderful happened in the garden. A horse can't live in a garden, but a mole can see everything.

Digger Mole

Helloooooo.

I'm Digger Mole.

I want to tell you about the morning something

wonderful happened right in my own garden.

Point to yourself.

Most of the time, I dig tunnels underground.

Dig like a mole.

I eat insects that might hurt the plants in my garden.

I try to dig carefully, but sometimes I bump

into a flower bed or chew on a carrot by mistake.

Then the gardener gets after me.

When I hear that the gardener is around,

I jump back into my hole in the ground.

Pretend to dive into a hole.

But on this special morning,

I was not underground at all.

That's because some strange things

had been going on in my garden.

Point to yourself.

I was sleeping deep in my mole hole

when I was jolted awake.

Open your eyes wide.

Something heavy was being rolled over my tunnel.

What was being rolled around

in the garden on a spring day?

Roll one hand over the other.

Then I remembered something

that happened a few days before.

The body of someone who died was put

in the cave on the far side of my garden.

Then a man named Joseph rolled a big,

heavy stone in front of the cave.

Make a muscle to show how strong you are.

And now that big stone was rolled off

to one side. I looked all around.

Shade your eyes to look around.

I didn't see any strong men

who could move the stone away.

There was no one in the garden at all.

Shake your head.

I was just going over to look in the cave

myself, when I heard someone coming.

It might be the gardener, I thought,

so I jumped back into my hole in the ground.

Pretend to dive into a hole.

But it wasn't the gardener. It was two men.

Hold up two fingers.

They ran over to the cave and

went in.

I walked over to the cave and looked

inside. My eyes opened wide!

How big can you make your eyes?

The cave was empty! *Empty!*

One of the men said, "Jesus is not here!

We must go and tell the others!"

The excited men ran out of the cave

and hurried back to the city.

Tap your hands on knees very fast.

What was going on in my garden?

Point to yourself.

I was headed back for my hole

when I heard steps on the garden path.

It might be the gardener this time, I thought,

so I jumped back into my hole in the ground.

Pretend to dive into a hole.

But it was a woman. She looked in

the cave and came out crying.

Touch your cheeks where the tears fell.

She looked all around in the bushes.

Look through your fingers.

She looked behind the olive tree.

I wondered if she had lost something.

I didn't know what she was looking for.

Do you know what she was looking for?

43

Then I heard the rustle of grass on the garden path.

This time it might really be the gardener, I thought,

so I jumped back into my hole in the ground.

Pretend to dive into a hole.

The woman thought it was the gardener, too.

She said, "I am looking for Jesus.

Tell me where you have taken him."

Jesus must have been the man

whose body was in the cave, I thought.

I peeked my head out just enough

to see what was going on in my garden.

Then the man spoke.

He smiled and said, "Mary."

Suddenly the woman knew who it was.

It was not the gardener at all. It was Jesus!

The man who had been dead was now alive!

Mary wasn't crying anymore.

Shake your head.

She was smiling.

Smile your biggest smile.

Something very wonderful happened that morning.

And it happened right in my garden!

Point to yourself.

A mole could not travel with the disciples, but a hound dog could hear everything.

Lop-along Hound Dog

Hello.

Bark.

I'm Lop-along Hound Dog.

I want to tell you about a big surprise.

Stretch your arms out wide.

Well, it was a surprise to the humans.

I knew it all along.

My master, Cleopas, and his friend had been staying

in Jerusalem for the Passover.

When it was over, we started to walk back home.

Tap hands on knees for walking.

We had to walk through some tall grass.

Rub hands together. Swish, swish.

I had to look behind the trees

to see if there were any snakes.

Can you wiggle like a snake?

Then we walked right through a little stream of water.

Splish, splash.

Once a chariot full of Roman soldiers drove past us.

I had to bark to protect my master.

Bark.

It was a busy day on the road to Emmaus.

But my master and his friend did not seem

to notice any of these things.

Shake your head.

Cleopas said, "So much happened this week!

First Jesus was a king with a big parade.

Wave your arms to Jesus in the parade.

Then the soldiers took him and he died."

Touch your cheeks to wipe away tears.

Quickly, I perked up my ears.

Touch your ears.

I remembered Jesus.

He had a kind word for everyone

and always had time to scratch me behind the ears.

Scratch behind your ears.

My master's friend said, "I heard that

some women have seen him again.

They say he's alive." Cleopas said,

"But we saw him die. How can he be alive?"

Shrug.

But before his friend could answer,

another man joined them on the road.

I started to growl to warn Cleopas.

Grrr.

Then I sniffed.

Sniff.

I knew this smell. This was someone

I had met before. But who?

Cleopas said to the stranger,

"We were talking about Jesus of Nazareth.

We thought he was the new king, but he died."

The stranger said,

"Do you remember what the Scripture says

about the new king?

It says he will not be the ruler of a new army.

He will be much stronger than that!

How strong are you? Make a muscle.

Anyone who believes in him will never die."

Shake your head.

This stranger sure knew a lot

about Jesus and the Scriptures.

I sniffed the stranger again.

It was definitely someone I knew.

I wondered if my master knew him, too.

When it started to get dark,

my master said to the stranger,

"Have supper with us. We can talk some more."

So we all went to an inn to eat dinner.

When the food came,

the stranger took the bread and thanked God.

He broke the bread in pieces

and gave some to the other men.

Pull your fists apart.

My master gasped, "Jesus!"

Yes! That was the smell.

It was Jesus! I knew it all along.

But as I looked up to bark "hello,"

Jesus was gone.

Snap your fingers.

We were so excited, we ran back to Jerusalem!

Tap your hands on your knees.

Back through the little stream of water.

Splish, splash.

Back through the tall grass.

Rub your hands together. Swish, swish.

When we got to Jerusalem, my master told everyone,

"Jesus is alive, and we have seen him!"

Hooray! Clap your hands.

I knew it all along!

Bark!

All the disciples wanted to see Jesus, especially Peter. A hound dog can't go on a fishing boat with Peter, but a cat can see everything.

Patches Cat

Hi, there!

Meow.

I'm Patches Cat.

My story is about the day

we ate breakfast on the beach.

My master's name is Peter.

We used to wake up early.

Yawn.

Then we took the fishing boats far out to sea.

Shade your eyes to see far away.

It was my job to catch the rats that sneaked on the ship.

Point to yourself.

If Peter didn't see any rats on board,

he gave me a fresh fish.

Rub your tummy.

I love fresh fish!

But one day, Peter left the boat and all the fish

to travel with a man named Jesus.

Wave good-bye.

I liked Jesus. He was a kind man.

He always knew where to scratch under my chin.

Purr.

Peter and Jesus didn't catch many fish,

but they told others about God's love

and helped a lot of people.

And I checked for rats.

One week, during the Passover holiday,

the city of Jerusalem was very busy.

Everyone was eating and dropping crumbs.

I had my paws full catching rats!

Suddenly, something bad happened!

Jesus was taken away by some Roman soldiers.

But instead of being a good friend to Jesus,

Peter ran away and tried to hide from the soldiers.

Later that night, as we sat by a fire,

a woman asked Peter, "Do you know Jesus?"

But Peter was afraid of the soldiers.

He said, "No, I don't know Jesus at all."

Shake your head.

Then a man asked him, "Do you know Jesus?"

But Peter said, "No, I don't."

Shake your head.

Another woman said, "Didn't I see you with Jesus?"

But Peter said, "I don't know who Jesus is."

Shake your head.

The next day, Jesus died on the cross.

Peter felt very sad and afraid.

But then Jesus was alive again.

That made everyone happy!

Smile really big.

Everyone except Peter. He was still sad.

One morning, Peter and his friends went fishing.

We fished for a long, long time.

Then I heard Peter say, "There's Jesus!"

Peter was so excited that he jumped into the water

and ran all the way to the shore.

Splash, splash, splash.

Now I don't like water very much,

but Peter had forgotten to give me my breakfast.

So I jumped in after him.

Splash. Swim, Patches!

When I got to the beach,

I heard Jesus say, "I forgive you, Peter."

Jesus knew that Peter was sorry for what he had said.

Now Peter was very happy!

Smile your biggest smile.

Jesus was alive, and they were still friends!

Jesus built a fire and cooked everyone breakfast.

I curled around Peter's legs.

Purr.

Peter said, "Well, Patches, are you hungry?

Would you like some breakfast?"

Meow, meow, meow!

Then Peter gave me a big fresh fish!

Rub your tummy.

I ate it in one bite!

Gulp!

I love fresh fish!

After that, the disciples spent all their time
telling wonderful stories about Jesus.
Most of all, they told everyone that Jesus
was alive again. What good news!

When we tell other kids the story of Easter,
that makes Jesus very happy.
Everyone who believes in Jesus
can live forever in heaven.

That's Good News for Easter and every day!